W9-CBG-014

DATE DUE

OCT - 3 2011	
OCT 1 4 2011	
NOV 2 8 2011	
JAN 2 5 2012	
MAY 2 5 2013	
JUN 2 6 2013	
AUG 2 1 2013	
NOV - 8 2013	
DEC - 5 2013	
OCT 0 5 2015	

Farley and the Lost Bone

by Lynn Johnston and Beth Cruikshank

Andrews McMeel
Publishing, LLC

Kansas City • Sydney • London

Andrews McMeel Publishing, LLC

an Andrews McMeel Universal company

1130 Walnut Street, Kansas City, Missouri 64106

www.andrewsmcmeel.com

11 12 13 14 15 TEN 10 9 8 7 6 5 4 3 2 1

ISBN: 978-1-4494-0-3065

Library of Congress Control Number: 2010943020

ATTENTION: SCHOOLS AND BUSINESSES

Andrews McMeel books are available at quantity discounts with bulk purchase for educational, business, or sales promotional use. For information, please e-mail the Andrews McMeel Publishing Special Sales Department: specialsales@amuniversal.com

For Farley Mowat

It was a perfect day in spring. The grass on the lawn was green, the breeze was soft, and the warm sun soaked into Farley's fur. It felt wonderful after the long winter.

Elly was outside, too. She hummed a happy song as she dug in her flower bed.

Seeing Elly dig reminded Farley of something.
Something he had wanted to do all winter. Something he
couldn't do while the ground was covered with snow. Now the
snow was gone, but Farley couldn't remember what he had
wanted to do.

Farley thought and thought.

What did Elly digging remind him of?
Was it . . . playing with the other dogs in the park?

No.

Was it . . . rolling in the cool, soft dirt to rub off the itchy fur he was shedding?

No.

Farley knew there was something he had really, REALLY wanted to do when the snow was gone. It bothered him that he couldn't remember.

Then he saw John pick up a wrench. He remembered! Elly had given him a big, juicy, meaty bone. He had buried it in the yard. That night, the snow had fallen and the ground had frozen. He hadn't been able to dig up his bone.

All winter long, he had dreamed about that bone. But where had he buried it? Farley couldn't remember.

He thought and thought.

Then he had an idea.

Maybe that's why Elly was digging in the flower bed. She was trying to find his bone for herself! Farley ran to the flower bed and started to dig. He had to find that bone before Elly did!

But he didn't find the bone in the flower bed. And Elly yelled
and chased him away.

Farley thought and thought.

Then he had an idea. Maybe the bone was under John's railway set!

But he didn't find the bone under the railway set. And John yelled and chased him away.

Farley thought and thought.

Then he had an idea. Maybe the bone was in Lizzie's sandbox!

But he didn't find the bone in the sandbox.
And Lizzie shouted and chased him away.

Farley thought and thought.

Then he had an idea.
Maybe the bone was in Michael's fort!

But he didn't find the bone in the fort.
And Michael yelled and chased him away.

Farley was sad. Everyone in
his family was mad at him.

He hadn't meant to bother anyone.
He just wanted so badly to find his bone.

Farley slipped away to his Special Place.
It was where he always went when he wanted to be alone.

Farley lay quiet and sad, not thinking of anything at all. The cool breeze ruffled his fur, and the sun sparkled and danced through the leaves around him. It shone brightest on a spot near him where the dirt was looser and the fallen leaves had been scraped away.

It looked . . . **it looked** . . .
like someone had been digging there last fall!

Farley jumped up in excitement. He dug and dug,
as fast as he could.

There it was! His bone! **NOW** he remembered
where he had buried it!

Farley danced out on the lawn to show the family his bone.

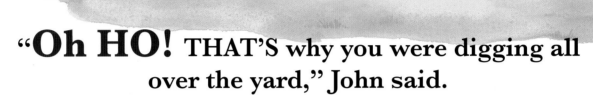

"**Oh HO!** THAT'S why you were digging all over the yard," John said.
"Aha!" Michael smiled. "I wouldn't have yelled if I'd known you were just looking for your bone."

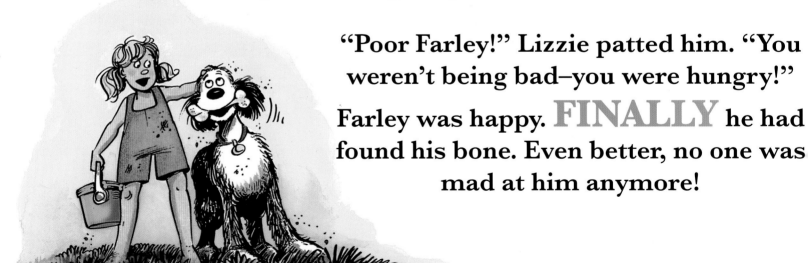

"Poor Farley!" Lizzie patted him. "You weren't being bad–you were hungry!"

Farley was happy. **FINALLY** he had found his bone. Even better, no one was mad at him anymore!

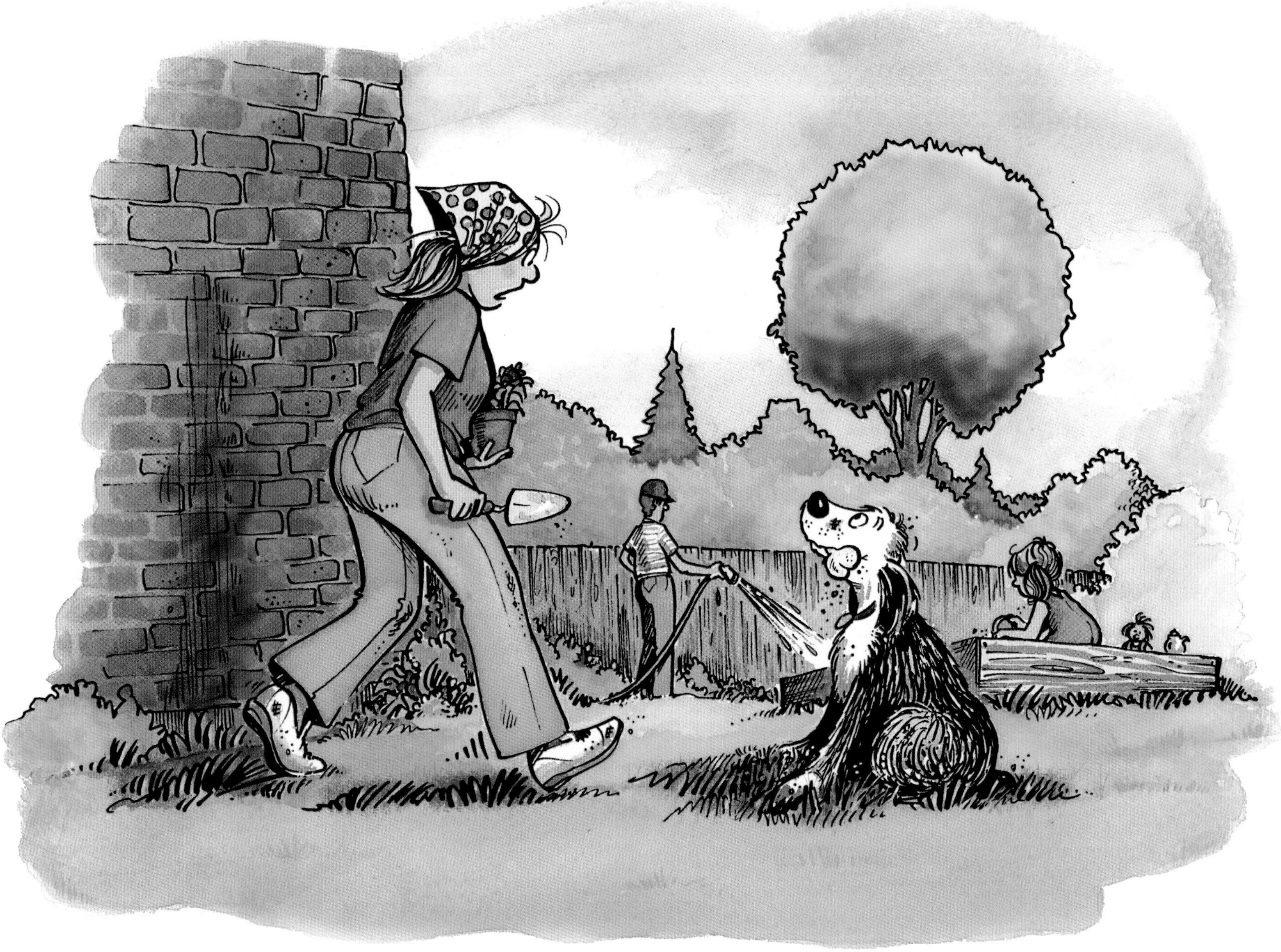

Then Elly came around the corner of the house.
"UGH!" she said. "That looks **DISGUSTING!**"

Farley agreed! It was the yummiest bone he had **EVER** had.
He flopped down to enjoy his treasure on the new green grass,
where the breeze was soft and the warm sun
soaked into his fur.

"Time for supper!" Elly called. Supper sounded like a great
idea to Farley.

But if he left his bone alone, someone might take it!
Farley decided to put his bone well out of sight. He dug a deep hole,
placed the bone inside, and covered it carefully. He knew it would
taste just as good when he dug it up again tomorrow . . .

or the next day or the next!

If he can just remember where he buried it!!!